STICK CAT

By tom Watson

Two Cats to the Rescue

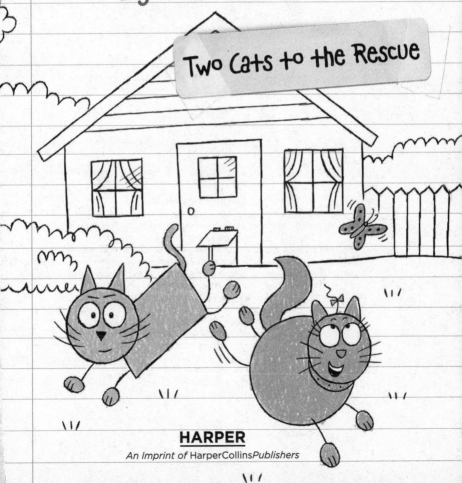

HARPER
An Imprint of HarperCollinsPublishers

Library of Congress Control Number: 2019936834
ISBN 978-0-06-274120-2

Typography by Honee Jang
19 20 21 22 23 PC/LSCH 10 9 8 7 6 5 4 3 2 1
❖
First Edition

To MEJ
(YGATB)

Table of Contents

Chapter 1A

MARY

So, you know who Mary is, right?

She's in my English class.

There are two things you need to know
about Mary.

1. She's totally into cats.

2. She's totally cute.

MARY LIST

1. CUTE

2. CATS

And there's one thing you
need to know about me.

1. I like Mary.

I wrote four Stick Cat stories for her to get her attention. It worked. She talked to me and walked with me to class and stuff. And, get this: she asked me to go to the Sweetheart Dance with her—where I totally impressed her with my amazing dance moves.

MARY

Now, it's almost the end of the school year and Mary's going to summer camp. And she wants me to write a new Stick Cat story so she can take it with her.

I said I would, of course.

What choice did I have?

She's totally cute.

(Tom: remember to tear out this chapter before giving it to Mary.)

Chapter 1

A NEW FAVORITE SPOT

In the big city, Stick Cat always woke up
before everybody else in the apartment.
He woke up before Goose, his roommate.
He got up before Tiffany, Goose's wife,
and Millie, their daughter. And he woke up
before Edith, his best friend.

He still wakes up before everybody.

But Stick Cat wasn't in the big city anymore.

This Saturday morning, while everyone else in the family slept in, Stick Cat woke up. He stalked silently from the bedroom, across the living room, and into the kitchen. A door in the kitchen opened up to the backyard.

Stick Cat loved, loved, LOVED that kitchen door. And here's why:

That kitchen door had a small swinging door at the bottom. It allowed Stick Cat and Edith to go outside and come inside whenever they wanted.

That kitchen door meant something super-important to Stick Cat.

Do you know what it meant?

I'll tell you.

It meant freedom.

He and Edith called that little swinging door
the Door of Freedom.

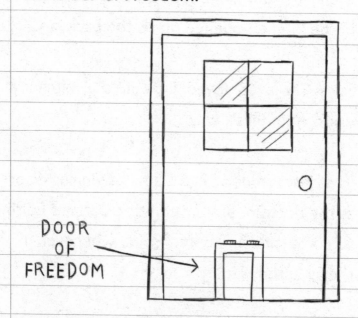

DOOR
OF
FREEDOM

Stick Cat pushed through the Door of
Freedom and emerged into the backyard.

He wasn't going to watch the big city wake up from a windowsill on the twenty-third floor of a tall apartment building.

He was going to watch his new neighborhood wake up from his new favorite spot.

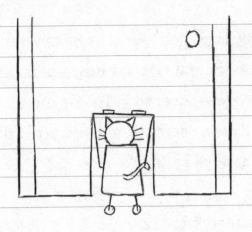

Chapter 2

THE MORNING—INTERRUPTED

Stick Cat gained speed as he crossed the back deck and hopped down onto the soft, green dew-covered grass. By the time he was halfway across the backyard, Stick Cat was at a full sprint.

He leaped into the air, dug his claws into a big maple tree's bark, and scrambled up the trunk. He passed a couple of the lower, thicker branches and kept climbing. Stick Cat was two-thirds of the way up when he reached his favorite branch. He stalked his way toward its end, found the spot where two smaller branches split off in opposite

directions, and lay down slowly
on his belly.

Stick Cat shimmied
himself into a
comfortable
position. He felt
the branch dip and
sway with his weight. He held
perfectly still until the branch settled.

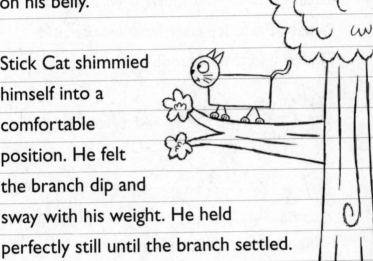

Once it did, Stick Cat took in everything
he saw.

In the big city, Stick Cat could only see
patches of sky between buildings. Here, the
sky went on forever.

He watched as
the sun rose and
brightened the day.

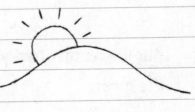

9

There was a park on a hillside in the distance. Stick Cat knew it was called Picasso Park. It was where Goose and Tiffany had their wedding party.

GOOSE   TIFFANY

After the wedding, Goose, Tiffany, Edith, and Stick Cat went back to the big city.

Millie was born about a year later. And about a year after that, their apartment began to feel too small. So, Goose and Tiffany decided to move to Goose's hometown and buy a house with a big backyard. The house was fine—and there was more space for everyone.

MILLIE

But it was that backyard that Stick Cat loved the most.

He scanned the neighborhood slowly from left to right. He saw the grass beyond their backyard fence. He saw the little patch of forest that was just past the grass. He saw several houses and an elementary school. He heard birds tweet, squirrels chatter, and dogs bark.

Stick Cat was about to scan the neighborhood back from right to left.

But he didn't.

There was another sound.

A sound he knew very well.

"Stick Cat!"

STICK CAT!

It was Edith.

Chapter 3

PUFFY TAILS ARE
NO GOOD

"Stick Cat!" Edith yelled again.

"Coming!" Stick Cat called back.

He hurried down the tree trunk, across the green grass, and over the deck. He stopped in front of Edith. She stood just outside the Door of Freedom.

"Is something wrong?"
asked Stick Cat.

"I'll tell you what's wrong,"
Edith answered quickly. "It's Saturday for

one thing. That means breakfast will be late."

"But Saturday breakfasts are always delicious. Tiffany and Goose cook together on the weekends. They have more time. They don't hustle off to work. They don't hurry to take Millie to preschool."

"That's all well and good," replied Edith. "But it's later, Stick Cat. *Later.* I'm hungry *now.* There's nothing worse than waking up without the smell of sizzling bacon or sausage in the morning."

BREAKFAST
TIME

Stick Cat nodded even though he didn't really agree.

"And here's another thing," Edith continued. "How is a girl supposed to get any sleep around here? I mean, jeez, can you believe all this racket?"

"What do you mean?" asked Stick Cat. He had found their new home in the suburbs to be quite quiet and peaceful at night. And Millie didn't cry in the night any longer.

"All this nature, that's what I mean," Edith huffed. "The incessant bird chirping, for one thing. It goes on forever and ever! The rustling leaves in the trees. Insects buzzing. Dogs barking in the distance. I swear. I even think I heard a babbling brook earlier. It all just drives me nuts!"

Stick Cat found this attitude hard to believe. "But the big city was way noisier."

"It's not the *amount* of noise or the *volume* of the noise," Edith explained. "It's the *kind* of noise."

"It is?"

"Most definitely," continued Edith. "I'll take car honks, rickety trains, and sirens over a bunch of birds and a babbling brook any day."

"I see."

"I mean, I only got thirteen hours of sleep last night, Stick Cat. What with all the commotion around here."

"I see," Stick Cat said again. "And thirteen hours of sleep is just not enough for you?"

"Not even close."

Stick Cat grinned at her. Only Edith, his best friend, would think thirteen hours of sleep was not enough.

"What are you smiling at, Mr. Man?" Edith asked with a mixture of curiosity and suspicion.

"Nothing. Nothing at all," Stick Cat said, and changed the subject. "Would you like to climb up into the maple tree with me?"

"Sure," Edith answered. "Maybe there's a squirrel up there somewhere. Nothing like a little squirrel-menacing to start the day—especially since breakfast isn't ready anyway."

"I forgot how much you dislike squirrels," commented Stick Cat as they padded across the back deck.

"Oh, I *despise* squirrels," Edith confirmed. A look of anger and disgust came across her face. "You know why, don't you?"

"No. Why?"

"Their tails, that's why," Edith stated as they stepped off the deck and into the grass. "They think their tails are sooooo special. *Pshaw.* They have a nice twitching quality, I'll grant them that. But that's the only thing I'll admit. Everything else about their tails is wrong."

"Like what?"

"They're all the same color and the same shape for one thing. I mean, how about a little variety, you know what I mean? And their tails are way too puffy. Tails should be thick and luxurious like mine. Squirrel tails are more air than fur. Imagine, just imagine! A tail that is more air than fur. It's bogus! Bizarre! Blasphemy!"

PUFFY TAIL

"Tails shouldn't be too puffy?"

"Absolutely not," Edith said, and gave her own thick tail a quick flick and flutter. "Thicker is better."

They reached the base of the tree trunk and were about to start climbing.

But they didn't.

They heard a sound from the house.
And Edith immediately lost all interest in harassing the inferior, puffy-tailed squirrels in the neighborhood.

When that sound came out of the house, Edith turned around and sprinted back across the lawn.

Chapter 4

KITTY?!

It was Millie. From inside the house she yelled, "Kitty?!"

Millie was Goose and Tiffany's two-year-old daughter. She could walk, talk, and giggle.

Millie could say five words—and a bunch of sounds.

Her five words were *Mama*, *Dada*, *binkie*, *Cat*, and *Kitty*.

Mama meant Tiffany.   MAMA =

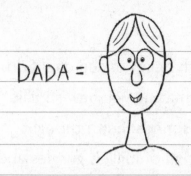 *Dada* meant Goose.

Binkie meant the small rubber thing Millie sucked on at night that made her go instantly asleep.

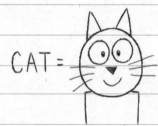 *Cat* meant Stick Cat.

And *Kitty* meant Edith.

So when Millie yelled, Edith came running.

Edith adored Millie.

That's because Edith believed she could do something totally amazing whenever Millie made some of her sounds. Edith thought she could interpret all of Millie's gurgles and noises. She could translate them. And her translations always ended up making Edith appear in a flattering light.

This part of the story provides an excellent example.

Watch.

"Come on, Stick Cat!" Edith exclaimed, hustling across the yard. "It's Millie! She's looking for me!"

"Okay," Stick Cat said, and turned toward the house too.

They pushed their way quickly through the

Door of Freedom and into the house.

Millie, wearing a yellow onesie, was in her absolute favorite spot—under the kitchen table. She loved to be under that table. She had a blanket under there. And she could stand up without hitting her head.

Edith rushed under the table and quickly began to circle Millie. She rubbed her left side against Millie as she paced around her counterclockwise—purring the whole time. Millie cooed and babbled and smiled.

And Edith translated her sounds for Stick Cat, who was now under the table as well.

"Do you want to know what she just said?" asked Edith.

"Sure," he answered.

"Well, first, she said good morning to me, of course. She's very polite, you know."

Stick Cat nodded. "Then what did she say?"

"She would like to know how I manage to make my fur so shiny and perfectly groomed first thing in the morning," Edith answered, and paused to take a short, studied look at herself. "Millie marvels—absolutely marvels— at my unique ability to present myself to the world with beauty and grace at such an early hour. She wonders how I do it."

Stick Cat did his best to suppress a grin and asked, "How *do* you do it?"

"It's not something that can be explained, to be perfectly honest," Edith replied. "It just comes naturally to me. It's actually quite a miracle."

"It certainly is," said Stick Cat. "Did she happen to mention anything about me?"

"Well," Edith said, and then hesitated for a couple of seconds. "I probably shouldn't say it."

"Why not?"

"It wouldn't be very nice."

"It's okay," Stick Cat said, still trying to keep that grin from appearing. "I won't mind."

"Well, she said your appearance is quite pedestrian and plain, I'm sorry to report,"

Edith said. "She sees many parts of your fur sticking up—and out of place. And your fur lacks the smooth, shiny sheen that mine has."

"She said all that?" Stick Cat responded. "In just that little time?"

"She did indeed," Edith said immediately. "Millie is quite the little chatterbox, as you know."

Stick Cat nodded and was thankful that he had, in fact, managed to hide that grin as Edith translated Millie's sounds.

He was also thankful that Goose and Tiffany walked into the kitchen. Just like Edith, he was hungry too.

He didn't know it at the time, of course, but Stick Cat would benefit from a hearty breakfast this morning.

He was going to need a lot of energy very soon.

The morning was about to get very busy.

Chapter 5

WHERE DID EVERYBODY GO?

"That was scrumptious,"
Stick Cat said after lifting
his head from his bowl
and licking his lips and
whiskers.

Goose made blueberry pancakes. Tiffany
made French toast topped with fresh
strawberries and whipped cream. There
was also a plate of bacon. The cats got two
strips each.

"It was okay, I guess," replied Edith as

she shrugged. She had finished her breakfast a minute or two before Stick Cat. "'Scrumptious' is a bit of an overstatement."

"Why's that?"

"First, the batter-to-blueberry ratio in the pancakes was off a good bit."

"It was?"

"Without a doubt."

"How so?"

"Well, I prefer a greater quantity of blueberries in my pancakes," Edith explained. "I like it to be about one-half blueberry to one-half batter."

"I see."

"And the French toast? Please," Edith said with clear dissatisfaction in her voice.

"What about it?"

"The whipped cream came out of a can, Stick Cat. A can."

"So?"

"Genuine whipped cream demands true effort."

"It does?"

"Yes," Edith said authoritatively. She knew her food—and did not lack confidence when speaking about it. "It's made correctly by pouring heavy cream into a chilled stainless steel bowl and then churning it frantically with an Italian-made metal whisk. It should take a good fifteen to twenty minutes. This so-called *whipped cream* this morning came from a can in the refrigerator. I mean, seriously. A can?"

Stick Cat peered down into Edith's empty bowl and saw neither a morsel of pancake nor a crumb of French toast. The bowl itself was shiny and wet—licked clean.

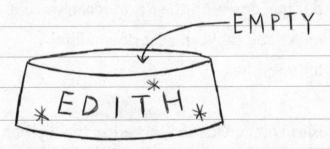

"Despite those faults—the small amount of blueberries and the whipped cream coming from a can—you seemed to enjoy your breakfast quite a bit," observed Stick Cat.

"Oh, don't get me wrong, I ate it," Edith replied. "But 'enjoy' is too strong a word."

Stick Cat was ready to change the subject. He was about to suggest to Edith that they head back outside to explore the backyard, but he didn't get the chance.

Right then, it got very busy in the kitchen.

Tiffany lifted Millie out of the high chair and put her down on the floor. Millie walked under the table and sat down. Edith followed her.   .

Meanwhile, Goose worked at the kitchen counter, scraping the leftovers into the smaller section of the sink. He poured the extra batter and pushed the broken eggshells and other stuff in there too. He turned the faucet on. Then he flipped a

switch on the wall and the disposal started
to churn.

Do you know what a kitchen disposal is?
Not all homes have them.

A kitchen disposal is a machine underneath
a sink. You push leftover food down the
sink, flip a switch, and the machine spins and
churns all those food things and water into a
liquidy mush. Then that mush goes down the
drain without clogging it up and making your
parents mad.

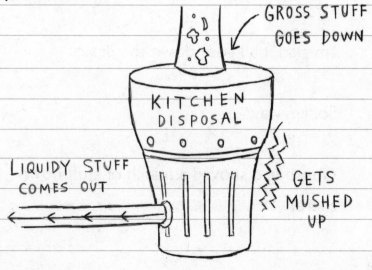

GROSS STUFF
GOES DOWN

KITCHEN
DISPOSAL

LIQUIDY STUFF
COMES OUT

GETS
MUSHED
UP

33

It's a pretty cool thing actually.

It can also be disgusting, now that I think about it. I mean, consider all the stuff that could be in there at one time. There could be eggshells, carrot peels, bread crusts, mayonnaise, baby food, eggplant, and a dozen other things in there all at the same time. And then the disposal machine slices, cuts, and spins it all into a gross, mushy, slushy mess.

Yuck.

I'm glad it all goes down the drain.

So, anyway.

Goose had shoved a bunch of stuff down there.

And that's when two things happened at the same time.

First, Goose flipped the switch—and then the sink disposal went to work.

And when a sink disposal goes to work, it's loud.

Really loud.

And it's super-loud if you happen to be the one standing at the sink.

That's where Goose was.

Then the second thing happened—Tiffany spoke.

"I'm going to run the errands now," she said from the kitchen doorway. Then she asked, "Can you keep an eye on Millie?"

But Goose didn't hear her at all—because of the sink disposal.

Goose looked down the sink and saw that the disposal had churned everything up and was empty now. Seeing the job complete, he said to himself, "Okay."

But Tiffany thought he meant, *Okay, I'll keep*

an eye on Millie when he was really saying
*Okay, all the food stuff is mushed up and down
the drain.*

Tiffany left to run her errands.

Goose spent two more minutes drying the
dishes and then turned away from the sink.
He called, "Tiffany?"

Nobody answered.

Goose looked around and saw only Stick
Cat. Edith and Millie were under the table.

"Where did everybody go?" Goose asked.

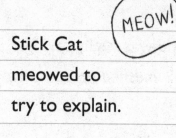

Stick Cat
meowed to
try to explain.

But Goose didn't understand that.

"Tiff?" Goose called again. And, again, he received no response. Then he snapped his fingers. "That's right. She said she needed to run errands this morning. She must have taken Millie with her."

And then Goose left the kitchen to go somewhere else in the house.

And a few minutes later, Millie left the kitchen too.

But she didn't go somewhere else in the house.

Chapter 6

UH-OH

"Uh-oh," Stick Cat said after joining Edith and Millie under the table. "I think there's a problem."

"What's that?" Edith asked. She was curled up near Millie's side. Millie was sitting. "Don't tell me Goose put that plate of extra bacon away. I'm planning on jumping onto the counter for a little midmorning snack later."

"No, that's not it. The bacon is still there," Stick Cat said, and then explained further. "I believe Tiffany thinks Millie is with Goose. And I'm pretty sure Goose thinks Millie is with Tiffany."

"Where's Tiffany?" Edith asked.

"She's running errands."

"Where's Goose?"

"He's in the house somewhere."

Edith shrugged and said, "It's no big deal. Millie can walk now. She'll find Goose when she wants to."

Stick Cat thought about that for a moment—and he realized Edith was right.

It wasn't anything to worry about. Millie could find her dad when she wanted to.

As if on cue, Millie pushed herself up and walked out from under the kitchen table.

"See, there she goes now," Edith said. Edith curled her body up some more to get into a comfortable sleeping position. She liked to take a nap after breakfast— and after lunch and dinner too. She closed her eyes and added, "Like I said, no big deal."

"I'm going to make sure she finds Goose," Stick Cat said, sounding relieved.

But Edith didn't answer.

She was asleep.

Stick Cat emerged from beneath the table.

He saw Millie right away.

She didn't go find Goose.

She went outside.

Chapter 7

WHERE'S MILLIE?!

Stick Cat saw just the bottoms of Millie's feet as she pushed through the Door of Freedom. The door swung behind her— and Millie was gone.

Stick Cat leaped back under the kitchen table.

"Edith!" he yelled.

Edith opened one eye halfway. She asked, "Yes?"

"You need to wake up!"

"How long have I been asleep?"

"Less than a minute!" Stick Cat said loudly and quickly.

"Well, you'll need to deal with whatever it is by yourself," Edith said before she yawned and closed that one eye again. "This is my nap time."

Stick Cat knew what to say to get Edith moving.

"It's Millie!" Stick Cat exclaimed.

He had never seen Edith move so fast.

Her eyes popped open. She pushed up to all fours with great force, leaping into the air. She landed and hurtled out from beneath the table. In two quick bounds, Edith was in the center of the kitchen. She snapped her head left and right frantically.

"Where is she?!" Edith screamed. "Where's Millie?!"

"Outside!" Stick Cat answered urgently. "She went outside!"

"How?!"

"Through the Door of Freedom!" Stick Cat
screamed and pointed at it.

Edith sprang toward the door and hustled
to it. She didn't push it open with her front
paws as she normally did. She BANG-ed her
head straight into it—never losing speed.
She was outside instantly. Stick Cat was
directly behind her.

And Millie was right there.

In the middle of the yard.

Sitting down.

Her head was tilted.

She smiled. She examined something on her hand.

"What is that?" Edith asked as they got closer. "On her hand?"

Stick Cat said, "It's a butterfly."

"Let's check it out!" Edith exclaimed joyfully as she bounded toward Millie and the butterfly.

And that's when everything changed.

Everything.

Chapter 8

A GAZELLE AND A FROG

The orange-and-black butterfly saw Edith coming.

It fluttered off Millie's hand and flew toward the backyard fence.

Edith chased after it.

Stick Cat chased after Edith.

And Millie chased after Stick Cat.

The butterfly flew over the fence.

Edith squeezed through the fence's wooden slats.

So did Stick Cat.

And so did Millie.

They followed the butterfly to the edge of the forest.

To you and me, it wasn't much of a forest, to be honest. It was simply a patch of a few dozen trees. In fact, you could see their house from anywhere among those trees. But to the cats, who had spent all their lives in the big city, it felt like a forest.

The butterfly landed on a lower branch of a sycamore tree. Edith stopped to stare at it, admiring its beauty.

So did Stick Cat.

And, even though Stick Cat and Edith didn't know it, so did Millie.

"That was fun!" Edith exclaimed. "Look how gorgeous it is!"

"It was," Stick Cat said. "It is."

And then someone said something they weren't expecting.

"Kitty!" Millie yelled. "Cat!"

Stick Cat and Edith jerked their heads around.

"Uh-oh," Stick Cat said.

"What's the matter?" asked Edith as she rushed toward Millie and began to circle her—rubbing and purring as she always did.

"Well, I don't think Millie should be out here, Edith," Stick Cat said.

"Why not?"

"Goose thinks Millie is with Tiffany," explained Stick Cat. "And Tiffany thinks Millie is with Goose."

"So what?" Edith asked as she paused to allow Millie to pet her.

"Neither of those things is true," continued Stick Cat and pointed toward their house. "We should probably get her home."

Edith nodded in understanding.

Then Millie made some sounds as if she wanted to take part in the conversation as well. She gurgled, grunted, and mumbled.

Edith cocked her head to the right to listen as she continued to circle Millie. She asked, "What's that, sugar?"

Millie made some more noise.

Stick Cat had to ask, "What did she say?"

"She just thought it was important to make a few observations about our journey here," Edith said casually.

"What did she observe?"

"Well, she noticed my leaping ability for one thing," Edith began. "She compared my athletic jumping to a gazelle on the plains of Africa."

EDITH =

"Did she compare my jumping abilities to anything?" asked Stick Cat. He couldn't wait to hear Edith's answer. He had begun to take real amusement in her translations.

Edith answered slowly, "I'm afraid so."

"And?"

"She thought, umm," Edith said, and waited.

Stick Cat suspected she was coming up with the comparison more than being polite. "She thought you were more frog-like."

"She compared my jumping skills to a frog?" Stick Cat asked. He was surprised. Frogs are, after all, excellent jumpers.

"Yes, but—" Edith said, and stopped.

"But what?"

"She said you jumped like a very *sick* frog."

"She did?" Stick Cat asked, and smiled to himself.

"Well, a very sick frog with a broken leg."

STICK $=$ CAT

BROKEN LEG

"Hmm," was all Stick Cat could think to say.

"It could have been worse," Edith said in an attempt to help Stick Cat feel better. "She might have said you jump like a very sick frog with *two* broken legs."

Stick Cat dropped his head to hide the smile on his face. He said, "Yes, I suppose that would have been worse, all right."

"So, really it was a compliment," added Edith.

"That's one way of looking at it," Stick Cat said, and raised his head. He had wiped that smile off his face. He was ready to change the subject. "We better get Millie home now."

"How do we do that?"

"I think it will be easy," Stick Cat said.
"You're her favorite thing in the world.
She loves you."

"What's not to love?" Edith commented.
"I mean, I'm graceful, beautiful, and I have
gazelle-like leaping abilities."

"Exactly," Stick Cat assured her. "I think if
you head back home, then Millie will just
follow you."

"Makes sense."

And that's exactly what happened.

Edith began to walk away from the forest and toward their backyard fence. Millie watched her—and took two steps to follow her.

But they didn't make it home.

Chapter 9

A GIANT MIRROR

After Millie's first two steps, the butterfly fluttered off that sycamore tree and flew into that small patch of woods.

It caught Millie's eye.

Millie stopped.

She stared at it.

And then she followed it.

Edith stopped and turned around. She yelled, "Millie! This way!"

MILLIE
THIS WA

But Millie didn't understand cat language. She just giggled, gurgled, and grunted. And she kept chasing that butterfly.

Stick Cat had stopped too, of course. He stood next to Edith.

"We have to stay with her," Stick Cat said quickly.

Edith nodded. "Wasn't that sweet what she just said?"

Stick Cat responded, "I can't, umm, understand what she's saying like you can, Edith. Remember?"

"Oh, that's right. I forgot."

"What did she say?"

"She said she absolutely loves chasing after beautiful things."

"That explains why she's going after the butterfly," Stick Cat said as they began to hurry after Millie.

"And?" Edith asked as they hustled side by side.

"And," Stick Cat said, and looked at Edith. He knew Edith better than anyone. And he knew how to answer. "It explains why she follows you around all the time."

"Exactly," Edith replied graciously.

The orange-and-black butterfly fluttered its way through the thin weeds and tree saplings at the edge of the forest. And Millie picked her way past a honeysuckle bush and crawled over a fallen tree branch. She never took her eyes off the butterfly.

And Stick Cat and Edith never took their eyes off Millie.

They scooched under, high-stepped over, and curled around everything in their path to stay close to Millie. Neither she nor the butterfly was moving very quickly, which gave the cats time to talk.

"We really need to get her turned around," Stick Cat said.

"I know how to do it," Edith said.

"You do? Great!" Stick Cat exclaimed, relief and excitement in his voice. "What is it?"

"It's perfectly simple, Stick Cat," Edith said calmly as they tromped through some cattail reeds. "We just need one thing."

"What do we need?"

"A giant mirror," Edith answered as they continued to track Millie and the butterfly through the woods.

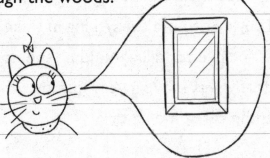

"Excuse me?"

"A mirror."

Stick Cat was grateful that the butterfly had chosen to land near the top of a small pine tree. Millie stopped too and stared up at it.

This gave him some calm time to ask Edith about her plan to get Millie back home.

His first question was an obvious one.

"Why do we need a mirror?"

"That's a silly question," Edith answered. "We need it to turn Millie around in the other direction, of course. That is what you want to do, right?"

"Yes," Stick Cat said, and scratched himself behind the left ear for three seconds. "I just, umm, don't understand how a mirror will accomplish that."

"Seriously?" asked Edith. She seemed genuinely surprised at Stick Cat's lack of smarts. "I mean, it's pretty obvious, Stick Cat."

"Maybe you could just provide some of your plan's details."

"Very well. If I must," Edith said, and sighed. "Since Millie is following the butterfly, it's not really Millie that we need to turn around. It's the butterfly we need to change direction."

This was, Stick Cat admitted to himself, a perfectly well-reasoned idea. He tried not to let the surprise show on his face.

"All beautiful things like to look at themselves," Edith confirmed. "You've seen me in front of a mirror many times, for instance."

"That's true."

"You take the giant mirror and strap it to

your back," Edith went on. "Then you position yourself beneath the butterfly. She sees her reflection and lands on the mirror to admire her own magnificence."

"Umm, okay," Stick Cat said slowly. "What then?"

"Then I jump on the mirror."

"You do? Why?"

"To admire myself," Edith said simply. "I'm beautiful too."

"Of course, of course," Stick Cat replied quickly. "Then what?"

"Then Millie climbs on the mirror because she wants to be with me."

"Of course," Stick Cat said again.

"Then you carry us home."

"I do?"

"You do."

Stick Cat just stared wide-eyed at Edith.

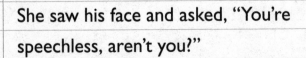

She saw his face and asked, "You're speechless, aren't you?"

He nodded.

"I'm not surprised you're in complete awe of me and my plan," Edith said proudly.

Stick Cat thought hard about the best way to respond. After a moment of careful consideration, he said, "Edith, it's the most unique butterfly-catching plan I've ever heard. I love how you and the butterfly get to admire yourselves while I carry the two of you, Millie, and the giant mirror out of the forest. Who else in the world would catch a butterfly that way? It's amazing!"

"I am quite special," Edith replied. "Thank you."

"You're welcome," said Stick Cat. He had decided not to criticize—or question—

Edith's plan at all. He had a different idea. He said, "I can't wait to get started. What do we do first?"

"We simply need to find a giant mirror," answered Edith. She seemed pleased that Stick Cat was so willing to adopt her plan.

"Sounds good," Stick Cat said. He began to look around on the ground.

Edith started searching about as well. In about twenty seconds, Edith asked, "Did you find one?"

"No."

"Did you check behind that little bush?"

"I did," Stick Cat answered as sincerely as he could. "And it turns out there is no big mirror behind that little bush."

"What about behind that dandelion?"

"Nope. No mirror."

"What about next to that pine cone?" asked
Edith. "Is there a great big mirror there?"

"I'm afraid not."

NO MIRROR

Edith emitted a great huff of disappointment.
This gave Stick Cat an opportunity.

"I'm upset too, Edith," he said, and lifted his head. "It's a shame we can't use your excellent plan—just because we can't find what we need."

Stick Cat then kicked at the ground a couple of times.

"It *is* a shame," Edith said. "But don't worry, I'm sure I can come up with another idea."

"I'm sure you can," Stick Cat said quickly. He was eager to put the Catch-the-Butterfly-with-a-Giant-Mirror plan behind them as fast as possible.

"Let me think, let me think," Edith said softly, and began to pace. She was already formulating a new strategy.

But she didn't get the chance.

Right then, the butterfly fluttered off that little pine tree and flew into the forest.

Millie giggled and chased after it.

Stick Cat and Edith chased after Millie.

And then everything changed.

Again.

Chapter 10

SQUASH-A-ROO!

"Where are we going?" Edith asked.

"Wherever Millie goes," answered Stick Cat.

As they moved through the woods, it grew more dense. The trees got bigger. The brush grew thick. The canopy of leaves and branches above them became more layered, blocking out more and more of the sun.

It grew darker.

And then it grew much lighter.

They—the butterfly, Millie, Edith, and Stick Cat—emerged into a small green peaceful meadow. Dandelions, daisies, and daffodils surrounded it. There was a big shallow puddle in the middle of the little meadow. There was a large rock in the center of the puddle.

The butterfly landed on a log at the edge of the puddle.

"Finally, we can rest," Edith said. "It's about time Miss Flutter-Pants took a little break."

Edith plopped down right where she was.

73

"I'm glad too," Stick Cat said after eyeballing Millie. She stood still, just staring at the butterfly. She was mesmerized by it. Stick Cat wanted to keep a close eye on her so he positioned himself between Millie and Edith before sitting himself. "It's so pretty here, don't you think?"

"It's more than pretty!" Edith exclaimed, looking around as she rested. "It's amazing! Just amazing!"

This response surprised Stick Cat. He didn't understand it. It was a lovely spot and everything. But it wasn't all *that* special.

"It's, umm, nice, all right," he said.

"Jeez, I thought you'd be more impressed," Edith said.

"With what?"

"With seeing *it* for the first time."

"Seeing what for the first time?"

"The ocean, silly!" Edith yelled joyfully, and pointed at the puddle. "The ocean!"

Now Stick Cat understood.

"You think that, umm, body of water is the ocean?"

"Of course it's the ocean," Edith said with sheer confidence. "I'm sure we'll see a dolphin or a whale or an octopus splash out of the water any moment now."

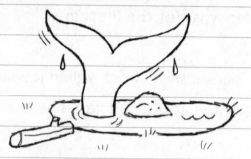

"Umm—" Stick Cat said.

"Which ocean do you think it is?" Edith asked before he could say anything else.

"Umm—"

"Do you think it's the Mississippi Ocean? Or the Jupiter Ocean? Or the Sahara Ocean?"

"I'm . . . not . . . sure," Stick Cat responded slowly. He decided it might be best to change the subject—and he definitely thought they should start steering Millie toward home. "We really need to do something about this butterfly. If Millie keeps following it, we'll never get her home."

"I think I know how to get Millie to quit following that butterfly."

"You do?"

"I do."

"How?" Stick Cat asked, glancing toward Millie.

"I think I should squash it," Edith answered simply.

"Squash it?!" Stick Cat exclaimed, and turned toward Edith.

"That's right: *SQUASH* it," Edith replied.
"I think I should saunter over to that log
real casual-like. And when Miss Flutter-Fuss
isn't looking, I'll sit on her. I'll give her the
old squash-a-roo!"

SQUASH-A-ROO!

"Edith, we can't squash the butterfly."

"Why not?" asked Edith. "She looks totally
squash-able to me."

"Well, first," Stick Cat began to explain.
"It's not very nice to go around squashing
things that are alive. It's kind of mean."

"Humph!" Edith huffed. She didn't seem
very convinced. "If given the opportunity, I'd
squash a squirrel in a heartbeat. Have I told

you about their annoying puffy tails? Puffy?!
That's nuts!"

"You have told me," answered Stick Cat.
"But, second, I think Millie
might get upset if you
squashed the butterfly.
She seems quite enamored
with it. She can't take her
eyes off it."

Edith shrugged the best she could while lying
down. She said, "Well, I don't want to upset
Millie. I would never do that."

"Good," Stick Cat said, happy that he had
quickly disposed of Edith's Squash-the-
Butterfly plan.

"Speaking of Millie," Edith said, looking past
Stick Cat. "What is she doing?"

Stick Cat snapped his head around. He hadn't realized how long their conversation had gone on.

Millie was no longer standing and staring at that butterfly on the end of the log at the edge of the puddle. She was belly-down on the log and scooting forward toward it.

The mud under the log was slick. And every time Millie scooted her weight forward to get closer to the butterfly, that log scooched forward and got closer to the water.

"Uh-oh," Stick Cat said, and leaped forward.

He was midair when Millie scooted a final time.

The log, the butterfly, and Millie slid into the water.

The motion startled the butterfly and it flew off. Millie watched it for a moment, but didn't seem to care. Something else had caught her attention. As she straddled that log, she felt the cool water on her fingertips and toes. She giggled.

Stick Cat landed and lunged to grab the end of the log and pull it back. His claws dug into its bark.

Then the bark peeled off.

And Millie began to float out to the middle of that puddle.

Chapter 11

TWO STICKS

Edith was right next to Stick Cat in a split second.

Together, they watched as Millie moved slowly out to the middle of that big puddle.

"No!" Edith and Stick Cat screamed in unison.

Now, if it was you or me, we would just step into that puddle and pull that log—and Millie—back to the grass.

But here's the thing: you and I are not cats. Well, I know I'm not a cat anyway. I guess you *could* be a cat. You know, like maybe you're a cat who likes to read books and that's why we're here together.

So, I guess we should find out.

Don't worry. This won't take long.

Okay, first go find a mirror. You know, in the bathroom or wherever.

Now look in the mirror. Do you have whiskers?

DO YOU LOOK LIKE THIS?

If you don't, then you're not a cat.

If you do have whiskers, then you *might* be a cat. Or I guess you could just be growing a really early mustache or something.

Anyway, let's assume we're both not cats. And, not being cats, we would just step into the puddle and retrieve Millie.

But here's the problem.

Stick Cat and Edith *are* cats.

And cats HATE water.

THIS IS WAY BETTER THAN WATER!

A cat would rather jump off a skyscraper than dip a paw into some water. I don't know why they don't like water. Maybe it's too cold or it messes up their fur or something. Whatever the reason, for this part of the story it's important to know that cats avoid water as much as I avoid lima beans.

Lima beans are weird.

So when Edith and Stick Cat saw Millie in the water, there was no way they could just splash out there and get her. Their instincts wouldn't allow them to do that.

They needed to think of something else.

"Okay, okay," Stick Cat said as fast and as calmly as he could muster. "This puddle is really shallow. If she slips off that log, she's big enough to just stand up. I don't think the water would be much higher than her ankles. She also looks pretty secure on that log all spread out like that. But we still need to get her. We can do this. I don't know how, but we can do this."

Stick Cat and Edith stepped around the dry edges of that wet puddle. The log had drifted and bumped against that big rock in the middle and stopped. Millie obviously wasn't going to just come drifting back, that was for sure.

While they tried to figure out a way to get her back, Millie was perfectly happy.

"She seems to be having a really good time," Edith observed as she and Stick Cat paced around the puddle. "She's talking a mile a minute."

It was true. Millie babbled and giggled as her toes dipped into the cool water.

Stick Cat asked, "What's she saying?"

"The usual," answered Edith. "She's remarking on my fabulous tail, finely coiffed fur, and overall smartness."

"I see," Stick Cat replied, and smiled. "I'm glad she's having fun, but we really should figure out a way to get her back."

"We could grab a bunch of boulders and throw them out into the water. You know, build a pathway out to her," Edith suggested. "We've got a head start. There's already one big rock out there in the middle."

"Umm, once again you've come up with a

really smart idea," Stick Cat said. "But
I don't see any boulders around here."

Edith was eager to come up with a strategy
that would work.

"We could fish her out," she said.

"Excuse me?"

"You know, get a fishing pole with a big hook
at the end of the line," Edith replied quickly.

"Umm—"

"We'd need to put some bait on the hook,
of course. Something she really loves."

"Bait? On the hook?"

"Yes, Stick Cat," Edith said. "That's how you

go fishing. Fish like to eat big, juicy worms and fat flies and tasty bugs and stuff. So you put some of that on the hook, throw it in the water, and then the fish bites it and gets caught on the hook. Then you drag it in."

"Edith, umm," Stick Cat said. "We don't have a—"

"Let me think, let me think," Edith interrupted, and paced a bit. "She loves peanut butter and jelly sandwiches. And macaroni and cheese. And edamame beans. And cucumbers. We can bait the hook with any of that stuff."

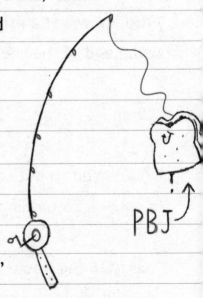

PBJ

"Edith, I don't think—"

"Stick Cat," Edith interrupted. "Do you have any peanut butter and jelly sandwiches, macaroni and cheese, edamame beans, or cucumbers with you?"

"No, Edith," he answered quickly. "And we don't have a—"

"Wait a minute! Wait a minute!" Edith interrupted again. She seemed excited about something.

Stick Cat hoped that maybe another—more plausible—idea had popped into her head. They needed a plan that might actually work.

"What is it?" he asked. "What did you think of?"

"We need to bait the hook with something that she absolutely loves, Stick Cat. LOVES!"

"Umm—"

"She loves me, Stick Cat! Me!" Edith exclaimed and jumped into the air. "We need to bait the hook with me!"

"What?!" he asked. He wasn't quite certain that he had heard her correctly.

"Quick! Get the fishing pole and the hook!" Edith said super-fast. "Then throw me toward Millie! She'll grab me because she loves me so much and then you can reel us both in! *Ba-Bam!* Perfect plan!"

Stick Cat didn't know what to say. Well, he knew what to say, he just didn't know *how* to say it. He decided simplicity is best.

"Edith, we don't have a fishing pole," he said.

"No fishing pole?" asked Edith. She seemed honestly surprised.

"No," Stick Cat said. "And I wouldn't want you swinging on a hook anyway. You could slip and get stabbed or cut. Hooks are sharp!"

"They are?"

"Definitely," Stick Cat responded, darting his eyes between the giggling Millie and the disappointed Edith. "And I couldn't cast you out to Millie anyway. I'm not that strong."

"You're not?"

"No."

"Maybe you should start working out, Stick Cat," Edith suggested. "You know, do some push-ups in the morning perhaps. Maybe do some strength training. Really work your core."

Stick Cat took a few—just a few—seconds then to himself. He looked down at his front paws, closed his eyes, and took a quiet, deep breath.

Upon raising his head and opening his eyes, Stick Cat said calmly, "You're right, Edith. I will, umm, start working my core."

"Couldn't hurt."

"And I'm sorry we don't have a fishing pole."

"It's okay," responded Edith.

"Millie's still out there," Stick Cat whispered.

"I see."

Stick Cat jerked his head right and left,
scanning the whole area for something—
anything—they could use. There wasn't
much there—just that big rock in the middle

of the puddle and some broken branches scattered about.

He looked toward Millie. She looked fine.

"Come on, come on," Stick Cat whispered to encourage himself. "You can figure this out."

"What's the matter?" asked Edith, overhearing him.

"We need to get Millie back," Stick Cat said. There was the tiniest hint of anxiety in his voice. "It makes me nervous to have her out of reach like this. I mean, I know she's safe and everything. In fact, it looks like she's totally happy. I just want to get her back—and get her home."

"It might be best to stick to my plan," Edith suggested.

"We don't have a fishing pole," reminded Stick Cat. "It's not possible to—"

And then he stopped talking.

He didn't stop talking because he was interrupted by Edith.

She didn't say another word.

He stopped talking because Edith had sparked an idea.

"What did you say?" he asked urgently, whipping his head around to Edith.

"I said it might be best to stick to my plan," she repeated.

He had it.

"'To stick to my plan,'" he whispered. "To stick. Two sticks!"

"What in the world are you talking about?" asked Edith. "And why are you repeating everything I say? It gets on my nerves."

"Two sticks!" Stick Cat exclaimed. "We need two sticks! You did it, Edith! We just need two sticks!"

Now, Edith definitely didn't know what her best friend was talking about at all. But that didn't matter. She was still happy to take credit for whatever it was.

"I really am quite clever," she said.

"You are indeed!" Stick Cat yelled happily. He raced about the edge of that small meadow, pulling on broken branches. "We need two long, strong sticks!"

Edith helped him look.

Stick Cat took one second to eyeball Millie in the puddle. She was fine—and still giggling.

Edith found one stick.

And Stick Cat found another.

"What do we do now?" Edith asked. "You know these aren't fishing poles, right?"

"Yes, I know," Stick Cat answered. Then he instructed, "You stand close to the puddle."

"I do?"

"Yes," he said, and backed up several steps, dragging his stick. "It's part of your brilliant plan."

"Oh, yes," Edith said. "Of course it is."

Stick Cat moved even farther back, only stopping when he reached where the woods began. He looked at Edith, who was now positioned at the edge of the puddle.

"Now what?" Edith called.

"You push one end of your stick into the ground and hold it upright."

Edith did exactly that.

"Now what?" she called again.

But Stick Cat couldn't answer. His own stick was in his mouth.

He eyed that water—that water that all cats don't like.

He squeezed his eyes shut.

He shuddered his shoulders—and then stiffened them.

He leaned back on his back legs.

He opened his eyes.

He saw the sunlight shimmer and shine on the water's surface.

He clenched that long, strong stick in his mouth.

And Stick Cat ran as fast as he could toward Edith.

And jumped.

As high as he could.

Chapter 12

FALLING IN LOVE?

Stick Cat soared through the air.
He clenched his stick in his mouth.

And he grabbed Edith's stick near the top,
sinking his front claws into the bark.

He pole-vaulted himself
across the puddle. There
was a solitary moment—a single
split second—when he felt
suspended and still above the water.
His heart skipped a beat. He did
not want to fall in the water.

And then he kept moving.

He let go of Edith's stick when he was directly above the rock in the middle of the puddle. He landed—safely and dryly—on the rock.

"Cat!" Millie squealed from the log.

He dropped the other stick from his mouth, smiled, and purred loudly at Millie.

"Stick Cat!" Edith called from the shore.

STICK CAT!

"Yes, Edith?"

"What are you doing out on that rock?"

"I'm going to use this stick to push Millie back to you!" Stick Cat called across the water. "It's part of your plan."

"Well, of course it is," Edith said, puffing her chest out with pride. "Duh."

Stick Cat picked up his stick, preparing to push Millie back.

"Hey, Stick Cat!" Edith yelled before he could start. "Guess what I just figured out?"

"What?" he answered fast.

"I can see my reflection in the puddle!" Edith said. She stared down at the surface of the water, tilting and turning her head to admire herself from several different angles. "Considering the adventure we've had this morning, I'm looking quite nice."

"Umm, Edith, I think we better—"

"Guess what else, Stick Cat?"

"What?"

"I think my eyelashes might be getting longer," Edith said dreamily, and fluttered her eyes to watch their reflection. "I've always had long, luscious eyelashes, of course. But it seems to me that they might be even longer and more luscious than ever before."

"That's, umm, great," Stick Cat answered quickly. He really wanted to get Millie back to dry land.

"You know what else I've noticed?"

"What?" Stick Cat responded hurriedly.

"This green ribbon really brings out the natural beauty in my eyes," Edith called across the water. As she raised her head to look at Stick Cat, she asked, "Don't you think?"

"Umm, sure. Most definitely."

"Hey, Stick Cat."

"Yes?"

"Why are you waiting so long to push Millie over here?"

"Umm, I guess I forgot why I'm out here," Stick Cat said. "Thanks for reminding me."

"No problem," Edith called. "It's good one of us is paying attention around here."

"I'm going to push Millie over now," Stick Cat informed Edith. "I'm going to do it real slow and smooth. I don't want to slip and fall in."

"What are you even talking about? Fall in what?" Edith called. "Fall in love? That's disgusting. How can you think about romance at a time like this? That's totally gross."

"No," Stick Cat said, and shook his head. "Not fall in love. I don't want to fall into the water."

"Oh," Edith said. She sounded relieved. "Oh, yes. That makes more sense."

Stick Cat used that long, strong branch to nudge the log—and Millie—off the rock. Millie giggled some more as she floated across the puddle toward Edith and dry land.

Stick Cat steered the log the best he could and gave it one final smooth shove.

The log slid halfway out of the puddle.

And stopped.

Millie looked up at Edith and joyfully yelled a single word.

"Kitty!"

Chapter 13

STICK CAT IS STUCK

With the butterfly gone and the cool puddle water no longer splashing her toes and fingertips, Millie turned her attention to Edith.

"Kitty!" she exclaimed, and scooched on the log until she reached its end. She climbed off it and joined Edith in the dry, green grass. "Kitty!"

KITTY!

Edith smiled, purred loudly, and rubbed against Millie's side, gently nudging her farther away from the water.

Stick Cat, meanwhile, stood on that rock in the middle of the puddle. He dropped his stick in the water and watched it float on the surface. He looked across the water. Edith purred and nudged Millie.

He got ready to jump across and join them.

But he didn't.

That span of water looked so much wider now.

The jump looked so much longer.

And Stick Cat figured out why.

When he jumped to the rock earlier, he had a running start. He had Edith's tall stick to carry him across. And he was motivated—

absolutely motivated—to get to that rock
and rescue Millie.

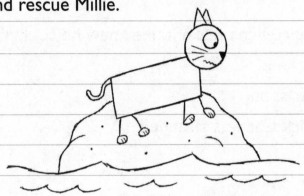

And Stick Cat knew something else.

He was lucky to have made it.

He didn't have any of those advantages to
jump back.

He couldn't get a running start.

He didn't have Edith's tall stick.

And Millie was now on dry land.

Stick Cat looked across the water again.

He couldn't make it. He knew he couldn't make it.

Stick Cat was stranded.

Chapter 14

A RUMBLING SOUND

Edith and Millie were comfortable and happy in the clearing. Stick Cat was glad to see that. He, of course, was still stranded alone on the big rock in the middle of the puddle.

"Stick Cat!" Edith called, noticing that he hadn't moved at all. "Why are you still out there? Are you going to go for a swim or something?"

"Umm—" he called back.

"Because if you're going for a swim, you're going to need some additional supplies," Edith yelled to Stick Cat before he could say anything else. "You need an inner tube, some sunscreen, and a bikini."

Stick Cat had to ask. "A bikini?"

"That's right," Edith continued. "I think so anyway. I don't know much about swimming. I can't stand water. I detest it! It's awful! It's evil! All cats loathe water!"

"Well, umm—"

"Hey, wait," Edith interrupted again. "I just thought of something, Stick Cat."

He asked, "What's that?"

"You're a cat!" Edith exclaimed. "You shouldn't like water at all. Why in the world are you going for a swim?"

"I'm—"

"I mean," Edith went on before Stick Cat could say another word, "I'm pretty sure you're a cat anyway. You've got the fur, the whiskers. You're fairly quick and agile. Oh, not nearly as graceful and athletic as me, mind you. But, you know, fairly catlike."

= CAT

"Edith, I—"

"You are a cat, right?" Edith asked. "And,

if so, why do you like it out there in that place? Surrounded by all that water?"

"I am a cat," Stick Cat responded as fast as he could. He didn't want to be interrupted anymore. "A cat I am. And I do not like this place I am."

"Oh, good," Edith said. She seemed honestly relieved to discover that Stick Cat was, you know, in fact, a cat. "So, what are you doing out there?"

"I don't think I can make the jump back," Stick Cat admitted. "I don't want to land in the water. I dislike water as much as you do."

"I have an idea," Edith called.

"You do?"

"Yes."

"What is it?" Stick Cat inquired hopefully. He was willing to try anything to avoid that dreadful water.

"Well, you're worried about not being able to jump all that way, right?"

"Right."

"Because you're concerned that you'll fall in the water, correct?"

"Correct."

"So, I know how you can do it."

"How?"

"You swim across," Edith said triumphantly.

She was quite proud of her idea, you could tell. "That way you don't have to jump at all!"

Stick Cat inhaled deeply and raised his head. He looked up at a few stray clouds as they drifted slowly by. After a long, calming exhale, Stick Cat lowered his head and said, "Edith, if I swim, then I'll be in the—"

He didn't finish his sentence though.

He was interrupted.

Again.

But this time it wasn't Edith who interrupted him.

There was a sound in the distance.

A rumbling sound.

It wasn't thunder up in the sky.

It came from the forest.

It was a growl.

A loud, menacing, angry growl.

And it was close.

Chapter 15

WHAT COULD IT BE?

"What was *that*?!" Edith yelled. She snapped her head to stare into the forest. Then she snapped her head back just as quickly to stare at Stick Cat. "Did you *hear* that?!"

Stick Cat, wide-eyed, stood stone-still on that rock in the middle of the puddle.

He had never heard such a ferocious, angry, guttural growl in his entire life. He had never

been in the woods before. And he didn't
know what lived out there. Coyotes? Bears?
Tigers? He had no idea.

He was startled.

He was frightened.

And he was motivated.

He had to get to Edith.

He had to get to Millie.

He didn't know what kind of terrible beast had generated and emitted such a threatening sound. But he did know one thing for sure.

If there was a growling, dangerous thing in the woods, he would do whatever he could to protect Millie and Edith.

A rush of energy flowed to his legs. A surge of adrenaline coursed through his entire body. He reared back on his hind legs and pushed off that rock with more strength and power than he had ever felt before.

He soared through the air.

He streaked over the water.

And he landed on the moist grass right at the puddle's edge with a safe and sloppy *PLURP!*

Stick Cat scrambled to join Millie and Edith.

"I did hear it," he answered, and panted when he arrived.

"What c-could it b-be?" Edith asked, her voice quivering as she spoke.

"I don't know," whispered Stick Cat. Whatever it was, he definitely didn't want it to hear them. "But I think we should try to get Millie home as fast—and as quietly—as we can."

Edith was all too happy to agree to this plan. She didn't want to find out what made that noise.

She wanted to get out of there.

Stick Cat wanted to get out of there.

But someone did *not* want to get out of there.

Do you know who it was?

It was Millie.

You see, she heard that ferocious growl too. But she was just two years old. She didn't know that ferocious growls were scary.

Millie wasn't frightened—she was curious.

And when two-year-olds are curious, they investigate. They touch things. They put things in their mouths. They explore.

As Stick Cat and Edith began to move *away* from that sound, Millie started to move *toward* it.

"No!" Stick Cat and Edith yelled together.

But it made no difference.

Millie moved even faster toward that scary sound.

In one minute, she saw what made that sound.

Stick Cat and Edith saw it too.

And they couldn't believe their eyes.

Chapter 16

A MONSTER SQUIRREL

Millie walked, stumbled, and hustled through the woods toward that growling whatever-it-was.

Stick Cat and Edith had no choice—they had to go along with her.

They stepped around and hopped over thick weeds, piles of scattered leaves, and broken twigs, sticks, and branches. In less than a minute, they came to an oak tree in another small clearing in the forest.

When they arrived, Stick Cat was happy to discover a couple of things.

1. There were no puddles here.

2. They were actually closer to their house. He could see it through the trees.

Two sounds came from that big oak tree as Millie, Stick Cat, and Edith stepped out of the woods and into the clearing.

RUSTLE!

GROWL!

The first noise was rustling. Near the top of the tree, some of the big oak's branches jostled and crackled.

"That's a squirrel!" Edith scream-whispered. "A terrible, puffy-tailed, chittering squirrel."

Right when she said that, the second sound came from behind the tree.

We already know what that was.

It was the growling.

The terrible, frightening, ferocious growling.

Stick Cat couldn't see what made that sound. He stepped in front of Millie. He didn't want her to advance any farther.

RUSTLE!

GROWL!

"Did you *hear* that?" Edith whispered. Then she pointed up into the tree at the rustling leaves. "Did you *see* that?"

Now, Stick Cat thought the rustling oak leaves and the growling sound were two separate noises.

But Edith did not.

"It's not just any squirrel!" Edith squeal-whispered. "It's a *monster* squirrel! The rustling! The growling! This must be the beast of all beasts! The brute of all brutes! A growling squirrel! I've never heard of such a thing!"

"I don't think it's a squirrel that's growling," Stick Cat whispered back as he continued to block Millie's way. She didn't seem to mind. She was curious and staring up at the rustling leaves too. "I think the growling is coming from behind the tree trunk."

Edith didn't pay attention to him at all.

"I mean, what would a monster squirrel even look like?" she asked. She pondered the idea. "It would have fangs for sure. Probably some extra-long and extra-sharp claws. Maybe that ridiculous puffy tail is covered with razor-sharp spikes."

"Edith, I don't think—" Stick Cat started to say.

"And I know one thing for sure about

monster squirrels," Edith interrupted. She
seemed quite sure of herself.

Stick Cat was compelled to ask. "What is it?
What do you know for sure about monster
squirrels?"

"I bet they have super-bad breath,"
answered Edith with complete confidence.
"Like really, really, really stinky, you know
what I mean? Like they just ate anchovies
and onions and old stinky socks. Yeah,
stinky breath for sure."

STINKY
BREATH

Stick Cat nodded. He didn't know what else to do.

"I'm glad you agree," whispered Edith.

Stick Cat wanted to get out of there, but they couldn't manipulate Millie or move her themselves. He could block her way a bit, but he couldn't actually change her direction—or make her move. And she was so, so curious about the growling sound and the rustling leaves.

Stick Cat didn't know what to do.

It was at that moment—that precise moment—when Stick Cat started to figure out what made that sound behind the tree trunk.

It was someone he had seen before.

Once, very long ago—when Stick Cat was a kitten.

And, again, at Goose and Tiffany's wedding party in Picasso Park.

At that moment, something emerged from behind that great oak tree's trunk.

It was a tail.

And Stick Cat recognized it.

Chapter 17

HIS NAME IS . . .

The tail was distinct.
It was long—and it had a puff ball at the end.

It wasn't a monster squirrel.

Stick Cat knew that tail.

It was a dog.

A dog he had seen before.

It was a poodle.

Stick Cat didn't know his name.

But I do.

And I bet you do too.

His name is Poo-Poo.

Chapter 18

BARKING

Stick Cat saw Poo-Poo's tail.

It's my turn to interrupt the story now. This will just take a minute.

You know who Poo-Poo is, right?

He's from the Stick Dog stories that I write for English class. There's a bunch of them—like nine or ten. The stories are all about five stray dogs who are always hungry and trying to sneak food from humans.

They've gone after hamburgers, frankfurters, pizza, donuts, spaghetti, and a bunch of other tasty treats. Stick Dog is the leader. The other characters are Stripes, a Dalmatian; Karen, a dachshund; and a mutt named Mutt.

And there's Poo-Poo.

Poo-Poo

He's a poodle—and he really, really, really doesn't like squirrels.

Okay, back to Stick Cat, Edith, and Millie.

"There's a dog behind the tree trunk," Stick Cat whispered. "That's who is growling. I think it's one of the dogs we've seen before. A poodle."

"A dog?" Edith whispered back.

"A dog."

"Not a monster squirrel?"

"Not a monster squirrel."

"I think we should try to leave here. *Quietly.*
Super quietly," Stick Cat added. His job right
now was to get Millie out of the forest and
back home. He figured a dog would only
complicate the mission. "Maybe if you start
walking toward home, then Millie will
follow you."

"Makes sense," Edith responded in a hushed tone. "I am her favorite, after all."

"That's right," Stick Cat confirmed.

Edith took one slow, silent step toward home.

But she didn't take a second step.

That's because right then, Poo-Poo circled the tree toward them. His head was fixed in an upright position, staring toward the top of the tree. An enormous growl raged from his mouth.

GRRR!

"He's growling at the squirrel up in the tree," Stick Cat explained. Poo-Poo didn't hear him. They were too far away—and Poo-Poo's full attention was on that squirrel.

"He doesn't like squirrels?!" Edith whispered with genuine enthusiasm.

"I don't think so," said Stick Cat. "That's why he's growling."

"I *love* this dog," Edith exclaimed. "If he doesn't like squirrels, he's okay by me! Maybe he finds their airy, puffy tails as utterly revolting as I do. Have I ever mentioned their disgusting puffy tails, Stick Cat?"

"You have, yes," he confirmed quickly.

"Well, let me just reiterate how incredibly distasteful me and this magnificent mutt find squirrel tails," Edith said, and took a great inhale of air. It appeared she was about to go off on another long speech about the awful attributes of squirrel tails. Stick Cat didn't want that. They didn't have the time.

But Edith didn't get the chance.

Right then Poo-Poo stopped growling.

He stared up into the oak tree.

And barked. BARK!

LOUDLY.

It was an angry bark.

It startled Stick Cat.

It startled Edith.

It made Millie giggle.

And then Millie did something totally surprising.

She barked back.

LOUDLY.

But it was not an angry bark.

And Poo-Poo lowered his head and jerked it toward them.

Poo-Poo stared at Stick Cat, Edith, and Millie.

And Stick Cat, Edith, and Millie stared back at Poo-Poo.

"Hello there, you marvelous mutt!" Edith called to him. He, of course, could not understand her. "I don't like squirrels either! Aren't their puffy tails ridiculous?!"

Then, to prove her disdain for squirrels, Edith looked up and *hissed* in the squirrel's direction.

Then Millie barked again.

Stick Cat had no idea what would happen next. Ideas raced through his mind.

Bad ideas.

Would that poodle charge right at them? Would he bare his sharp teeth and snarl? Would he attack?

Stick Cat felt the fur on the back of his neck stand up a bit. He felt his claws emerge slightly from his paws.

And then Poo-Poo moved.

He took action.

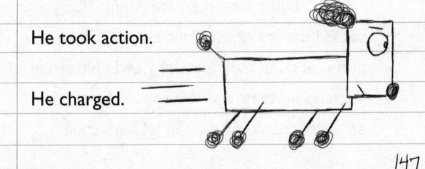

He charged.

Chapter 19

ANOTHER EDITH PLAN

Poo-Poo charged.

Into the forest.

"Wait!" Edith screamed after him. "Come back! I don't like squirrels either! Those puffy tails! All that twitching and chittering! We should team up! We should form an unstoppable Anti-Squirrel Squadron!

With your fierce growling and my grace, athleticism, beauty, magnificence, style, elegance, strength, smarts, charm, and, most of all, modesty, we could soon eradicate the squirrels in this neighborhood forever! We'd never see a squirrel again! Come back! Oh, please, come back!"

While Edith called and pleaded for Poo-Poo's return, the fur on the back of Stick Cat's neck collapsed back down to its natural, comfortable position. He relaxed a little and breathed easier.

He knew the poodle was long gone. Upon seeing them, that dog had instantly sprinted away from the big oak tree, hurtled over some brush on the other side of the little clearing, and raced through the woods.

"I don't think he's coming back," Stick Cat said to Edith. There was relief in his voice.

"He's not?" Edith asked, turning to him.

"I don't think so."

"But if he doesn't come back, how will we combine our strengths to create the Anti-Squirrel Squadron?" Edith asked. She seemed honestly distressed.

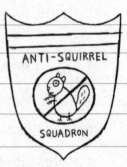

"I don't know," Stick Cat said, shaking his head. He decided then to refocus Edith— and himself—on their mission. "Maybe we'll see him again someday though. Right now,

however, I think we better figure out a way
to get Millie back home."

Edith then turned away from that spot in the
forest where the poodle had disappeared.
She turned toward Millie, who babbled,
gurgled, and smiled at her.

"Yes, we should," Edith said, and stepped
closer to Millie. She rubbed her left side
against Millie and purred loudly. "I know how
to do it."

I KNOW HOW TO DO IT.

"You do? How?"

"Well," Edith began as she continued to
circle Millie and rub gently against her.

"We're trying to get her back to the house, right?"

"Right."

"But we can't get her to move in that direction, right?"

"Right."

"So just turn it around."

Stick Cat hesitated for a single moment before asking, "Turn what around?"

"The whole problem."

After a slightly longer pause, Stick Cat said, "I'm not quite following you, Edith."

"Well, since we can't bring *Millie* to the *house*," Edith explained proudly. "We simply bring the *house* to *Millie*! *Ba-BAM!* Problem solved!"

"We bring the house to Millie?" asked Stick Cat. He tried to say it calmly, but this was a nutty idea—even for Edith.

"Well, not *we*, specifically," answered Edith. "More like *you*. *You* bring the house to Millie. I'm staying here."

"You're staying here?"

"That's right," Edith explained. "I'm kind of tired. It's been a busy day, you know. What with rescuing Millie from the puddle, coming up with all these ideas by myself. I'm also trying to get the Anti-Squirrel Squadron started. I'm beat. You go on and get the house. Millie and I will find a nice spot of shade and wait for your arrival. Might take a nap."

"You'll take a nap while I, umm, bring back the house?"

"Right you are, Stick Cat," Edith responded. She looked around for a comfortable shady area. "I'm glad you understand."

"Edith, I can't—"

"You know, I think it might be nice to have the house out here in the forest," Edith interrupted. "Lots of trees to climb. Plenty of squirrels to feel superior to. Nice cool shade. I could do without some of the noise. As I've mentioned previously, that babbling brook can be awfully annoying when I'm trying to sleep. But, overall, it might be a nice location."

"It, umm, would be nice here, I suppose," said Stick Cat. "But, Edith, I can't—"

"Yes, yes," Edith interrupted once more. "The idea of locating our house here really works for me. Let's do it. Off you go, Stick Cat. Off you go."

"Off I go where?"

"To get the house, silly," Edith said. "How

long do you think you'll
be? Twenty minutes?
Thirty? An hour?"

"Edith—"

"Try not to be more than an hour," said
Edith. "I'm getting hungry. It must be getting
close to lunchtime. When you bring the
house, don't forget to bring the kitchen.
Very important to bring the kitchen. That's
where the food is, you know."

"Yes, I know. But Edith—"

"I wonder what Tiffany is making for
lunch today," Edith said, and licked her
lips. "Cheese tortellini in a puttanesca
sauce sounds yummy, doesn't it? I suppose
some thinly sliced sirloin cooked medium
rare might suit. Maybe a side of fingerling

potatoes dusted with finely grated Parmesan cheese. I'm getting hungry just thinking about lunch."

"Edith, I—"

"Stick Cat, can I ask you a question?"

"Umm, sure."

"Why are you still here?" Edith inquired, not unkindly. "I mean, the house is not going to move itself."

"Edith," Stick Cat said as fast as he could. "I can't bring the house here. It's far too heavy. It must weigh tons. I could never lift it in a million years."

"You can't lift the house?" she asked, honestly surprised.

"No."

Edith was silent then for a moment. She thought about something. After that brief period of pondering, she spoke.

"Don't worry about it, Stick Cat," she said. "It's no big deal."

"It's not?" replied Stick Cat. It seemed strange to him that she gave up on her idea so quickly.

"No, it's not," Edith repeated. "No big deal at all."

"That's great. Then maybe we can figure out another way to—"

"Instead of *lifting* the house, you can just *push* it," Edith interrupted.

"What?"

"You can push it instead," Edith repeated.
She turned her head left and right, renewing
her search for a cool, comfortable, shady
area.

"*Push* the house?" Stick Cat asked. "You
want me to *push* the house?"

"Sure," Edith said. "Everybody knows that
pushing things is way easier than *lifting*
things."

"Edith, I can't—"

"You'll need to wind your way through some of the bigger trees, of course," added Edith. "But the smaller stuff—the saplings and the bushes—you should be able to plow right over. Easy stuff. See you later. Don't forget the kitchen."

Stick Cat would have explained that pushing the house through the forest was just as impossible as lifting and carrying the house through the forest.

But he did not get the chance.

At that precise moment, two more sounds emerged.

This time, it was not the rustling of leaves created by a squirrel.

And it was not the powerful and fierce growling of Poo-Poo.

There were two completely different sounds.

One of the sounds they had heard before many times.

The other sound they had never heard before in their lives.

Chapter 20

SOMETHING IS COMING

Millie whimpered.

That was the first sound. It was the sound
Millie made before crying—and the cats
knew it.

"Oh no, Stick Cat," Edith
exclaimed. "Millie! She's
going to cry soon!"

Stick Cat nodded. He had
heard that whimpering sound too.

Edith began to circle Millie more quickly,

rubbing against her even more for reassurance. Edith asked, "What do you think is wrong?"

"It could be anything," replied Stick Cat. "We've been out here a long time. She could be hungry. She could be sleepy. She might be missing Goose and Tiffany."

"She's probably not missing her parents," Edith partially disagreed. "I'm right here, after all. And I'm her favorite."

Stick Cat smiled a bit to himself then.

"But she could be sleepy or hungry," Edith continued. "That's possible. Do you have any food with you? I could eat some and then share the leftovers with Millie."

"Food?"

"Yes, food. You know, the stuff you eat," Edith confirmed and explained. The idea that Stick Cat might have carried some food from the house with him seemed perfectly logical to her. "Some filet mignon perhaps? Maybe a lobster bisque? Even some bagels with lox and cream cheese would suffice. That would be enough to hold us over before we get home."

"Umm, no, Edith," Stick Cat replied. "I didn't bring any food with me."

"Why don't you just bring us something from

the kitchen?" asked Edith. "Didn't you bring
the kitchen when you brought the house?
I seem to remember mentioning the kitchen
quite specifically. It was part of my plan."

"Umm. It was part of your plan, yes," Stick
Cat answered. "But that, umm, didn't quite
work out."

That's when the second sound emerged.

It was faint at first, nearly lost among all the
other sounds in the woods—insects, birds,
and rustling leaves.

It was a rumble.

RUMBLE!

A quiet rumble.

But it grew louder quickly.

Edith heard it too. She glanced up at the sky.

"Is that thunder?"

"I don't think so," Stick Cat answered slowly. The rumble was already louder. It was already closer. He felt the ground beneath his paws tremble. The sound didn't come from the sky—it came from the forest.

"Then what is it?"

"Something's coming," Stick Cat whispered. He took five quick steps to put himself between that growing, rumbling sound and Edith and Millie. "Something is approaching. Fast! Something is charging toward us!"

SOMETHING'S COMING.

Edith said, "It might be a rhinoceros. Those things charge."

Stick Cat listened more closely.

"There's more than one," he whispered.

"I've always wanted to see a rhinoceros," Edith said. "They're so big. And their skin is folded over. And that horn? That horn is awesome. Do you think it could really be more than one rhinoceros?!"

"It's more than one something," Stick Cat said. He snapped his head around, seeking a place to hide. They were in the open in this little clearing. He knew they couldn't get Millie to move. And whatever was coming at them was moving rapidly.

The sound was louder.

The ground trembled more.

Branches, bushes, and tall weeds swayed and snapped as the things got closer.

"Maybe it's an entire herd of rhinoceroses!" Edith exclaimed. "Wouldn't that be wonderful!"

And then the things emerged from the forest on the opposite side of that clearing.

Chapter 21

MAGICAL FAIRIES

It was not a rhinoceros.

It was not a herd of rhinoceroses.

It was the poodle.

And four other dogs.

Along with Poo-Poo, there were Stick Dog, Mutt, Karen, and Stripes. They stopped at the edge of that clearing.

The five dogs stood absolutely still and stared at the two cats and Millie. And the cats and Millie stood absolutely still and stared at the five dogs.

And then everybody started talking at once.

The dogs began to assess the situation.

The cats, obviously, could not tell what the dogs were barking and talking about.

But you and I can.

And here's what they said.

"See? I told you they'd be here," Poo-Poo

said. He was proud—and a little nervous—
about his discovery.

"But who are they?" asked Stripes. "And
what are they doing here?"

"I think I know,"
said Karen.

"You do?" Stick Dog
asked.

"The cats aren't really cats at all," suggested
Karen. "I think they're more like woodland
fairies and forest sprites. You know, magical
creatures."

"What do you mean, Karen?" Mutt asked.

"I've always thought the woods are full
of fairies," Karen explained. "They take

care of things around here. They help the trees, bushes, and mushrooms grow. They sprinkle magical dust all about, creating sparkling clouds that float and drift all over the forest. When some of that dust lands on something, that thing will grow and flourish—or even transform into something new and magical!"

Poo-Poo, Stripes, and Mutt listened to
Karen intently. They were fascinated with
her theory—and appeared to believe it.

Stick Dog was not quite so sure.

He asked, "So you think these two cats are
magical fairies?"

"What else could they be?" Karen asked,
and nodded. "I mean, what do you think
they are, Stick Dog?"

"I, umm, think they're cats."

But nobody really heard him because Stripes
started talking at the same time.

"Karen, I understand that the cats are
actually woodland fairies who keep the
woods alive and thriving," she said. "But

what about the little human? Where did she come from?"

"She must be the result of a magical fairy-dust transformation. She must have been something else before," Karen replied. She seemed to be an expert on the subject. "I think that little human was a dandelion before. Yes, a dandelion. The woodland cat fairies sprinkled some magic dust on a dandelion and—*POOF!*—up popped this little human! Makes perfectly good sense."

Stripes, Mutt, and Poo-Poo all nodded their heads in understanding. Apparently, it made perfectly good sense to them too.

It did not, however, make perfectly good

sense to Stick Dog. And he believed it was now time to get his friends to look at things more realistically. He eyed the little human for a few seconds. She looked distressed. He thought she might be about to cry.

"You guys," he said a little louder than usual. His voice was not unkind, but there was the tiniest hint of authority in it. "This idea that the, umm, woodland cat fairies sprinkled magical dust on a, umm, dandelion to grow this little girl is fascinating. But I have a different thought."

"Here it comes," whispered Karen to Stripes, Poo-Poo, and Mutt. It was still plenty loud enough for Stick Dog to hear though. "Old Stick Dog is about to go off on another of his crazy tangents. What kind of nutty idea will he come up with this time, do you think?"

Stick Dog pretended he didn't hear this and went on.

"I think this whole situation might have a more logical explanation," he said. "I think this little human wandered into the woods and the cats are trying to help her get home. I think there's a pretty good chance that they live together."

Mutt, Stripes, Poo-Poo, and Karen all tilted their heads a bit to the left as they considered this idea.

With a smile, Stick Dog added, "There's something else I want to mention as well."

"What's that, Stick Dog?" asked Mutt.

"We've seen these cats before," Stick Dog explained. "We saw the male cat when he was a kitten at the Pizza Palace years ago. Then a couple of summers ago we saw them both at that wedding party at Picasso Park. Remember? We got barbecue ribs, mashed potatoes, and cake."

Karen asked, "Do you think they have any of that wedding cake with them?!"

"Umm, I doubt it," answered Stick Dog.

It was then—and only then—that Stripes realized who she was looking at. She snapped her head to stare at Stick Cat. Recognition—and adoration—flashed onto her face.

"My soul mate!" she screamed.

Stripes used all her strength, speed—and pure delight and utter happiness—to leap across the clearing in five joyful bounds.

She headed right toward Stick Cat.

Chapter 22

HERE COMES STRIPES

While the dogs talked among themselves, the cats did the same thing.

The dogs, of course, could not tell what the cats were meowing and talking about.

But you and I can.

And here's what they said.

Edith sighed a bored and exasperated sigh.

SIGH.

She said, "I don't know if I've ever been more disappointed in my entire life."

Stick Cat did not expect such a comment from Edith. He thought she would be shocked, nervous—even frightened. That's the way he felt. He had no idea what would happen next. He kept a constant eye on the dogs. He didn't believe they were in a threatening posture. They seemed more curious than anything. But he didn't want to take any chances. He watched them very closely.

"You're disappointed?" he asked.

"Totally."

"Why?"

"These are five dogs, Stick Cat. Dogs," Edith explained. "They are not rhinoceroses at all. It's just disappointing."

"Umm, well. Yes. I can see why you're disappointed," replied Stick Cat. "But the good news is that I'm pretty sure these dogs are friendly."

"How do you know?"

"Well, I think we've seen them before," explained Stick Cat. "On Goose and Tiffany's wedding weekend. Remember?"

A flash of recognition came to Edith's face then. She did remember.

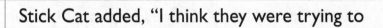

Stick Cat added, "I think they were trying to

get the leftover barbecue ribs and mashed potatoes at the party. They're strays, I think. They're always hungry."

Edith nodded. She remembered something specific just then.

"That's right. I remember," Edith said. "And the spotted one is totally hyper, right? She was obsessed with you or had a crush on you or some bizarre thing like that. Right?"

"That's right," Stick Cat said, turning away from the dogs for the first time and toward Edith. He smiled and added, "She did act a little strange toward me."

It was then—when Stick Cat turned briefly to Edith—that the Dalmatian barked. From across the clearing, Stripes yelped, "My soul mate!"

She bounded across the clearing with great speed, complete glee, total enthusiasm, and sheer affection.

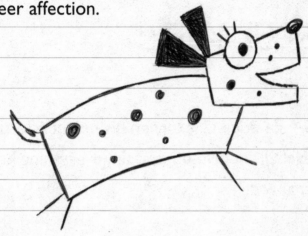

It took her five great bounds to reach Stick Cat.

He never saw her coming.

And then Stripes did something totally unexpected.

Chapter 23

SOUL MATES

When Stick Cat turned his head back to eyeball the five dogs again, everything had changed.

He could not see five dogs.

He could only see one dog.

A white dog with black spots.

Stripes.

She plummeted haphazardly out of the air.

Right at Stick Cat.

And Stick Cat had less than
one-half of one second to
decide what to do. He could
poke his claws out of his paws.
He could swat and scratch at
her. That's what his instincts
told him to do.

But, thankfully, Stick Cat did not listen to his
instincts.

He had a feeling these dogs might be able to
assist them—might be able to help them get
Millie back home safely.

Stick Cat held still.

And Stripes landed six inches short of where
he stood, skidded five inches, and stopped.

She wrapped all
four of her legs
around him in a tight,
wondrous hug.

She screamed,
"My soul mate!"

Stick Cat didn't know what to do. The
Dalmatian's delighted expression signaled
that she was not threatening at all. Her eyes
were welled up with joyful tears. A goofy,
overwhelmed smile spread across her face.

Still, Stick Cat didn't really like being
squeezed that hard.

He wriggled gently out of her grasp, but did
not move away from her. Instead, he ducked
his head a little and brushed his left side
across her chest, purring as he did.

Stripes yelped with joy.

"He likes me!" she screamed as Stick Cat rubbed her and purred. "My soul mate really likes me!"

HE LIKES ME!

Something about this joyful interaction between Stripes and Stick Cat seemed to wash across the entire group. A sense of calm and companionship was in the air.

"I'm sure these dogs are friendly," Stick Cat said to Edith.

"I think so too," she replied. "Plus we know the poodle has a deep dislike for squirrels. That alone makes me admire him. I can't stand those puffy-tailed varmints! Have I ever told you about their ridiculous tails?"

"Yes," Stick Cat said quickly.

"Did you see that, you guys?" Stripes asked her friends. Mutt, Karen, Poo-Poo, and Stick Dog had all moved away from the edge of the clearing and come closer. "My soul mate feels the same way about me! He made the nicest, warmest, vibrating sound when he rubbed against me! It was so welcoming! For a moment we were one being—alone and content together in the vastness of the universe!"

"That's, umm, great, Stripes. Really great," Stick Dog said. He wasn't quite as certain that the male cat had expressed himself as her soul mate. But he did think it was a kind and welcoming gesture.

"Yeah, I like these cats," agreed Poo-Poo. "The fancy one—the female—really doesn't like squirrels. You should have heard the angry hissing she aimed up at a squirrel earlier. It was totally mean. I loved it! Anyone who acts that way toward those chittering, nasty, tail-twitching, acorn-dropping villains is okay in my book!"

These conversations of mutual respect and admiration might have continued for a little while longer.

But they didn't.

Right then, Millie whimpered again—this time louder.

Chapter 24

MUTT SHAKES

"What should we do, Stick Cat?!" Edith asked. All her attention was instantly refocused on her favorite person, Millie.

Stick Cat didn't know what to do. He just shook his head.

But the cats were not the only ones there. The dogs had also noticed Millie's welled-up eyes, her sad expression, and her whimpering sounds.

"Stick Dog, something's wrong with that little human," Karen said.

"I can tell," he replied, having noticed too.

"What should we do?" asked Stripes.

"I don't know," said Stick Dog honestly. "I mean, we're stray dogs. All we do with humans is try to take their food. I don't know how to actually interact with them— let alone solve this little one's problems."

"We see little humans at Picasso Park all the time," Poo-Poo said. He had thought of something. "They're usually playing with something. You know, like a ball or a Frisbee or a toy. Maybe we could give her a toy."

Stick Dog twitched his head a little.
This idea, he thought, had potential. He
whispered, "Interesting."

Stripes asked, "Is there a toy store anywhere
around here?"

"In the middle of the woods?" asked Stick
Dog. He was certain there was no toy
store in the woods. He was also certain that
they couldn't go buy a toy if there was one.
They didn't have any money. And, you know,
they were dogs. Stores were for humans.

"Sure, why not?" responded Stripes.
"There's lots of other stuff around. Trees,
bushes, birds, leaves, weeds, branches. Why
not a toy store?"

"Umm—" said Stick Dog.

"Yeah, Stick Dog, why not a toy store?"
Karen interrupted. "You need to have a
more positive outlook. Stop being such a
Debbie Downer! Let's really *believe* that
there's a toy store out here in the forest!
Let's wrap that toy store in positive mental
energy! Let's *trust* that it's there!"

This pep talk energized Mutt, Poo-Poo, and
Stripes. They turned their heads this way
and that way. They squinted their eyes and
peered in every direction.

They didn't find a toy store.

"Okay, so Stick Dog was right," Karen admitted after about twelve seconds of searching. "There's no toy store in the middle of these woods. But don't we all feel better—don't we all feel more positive— about there *not* being a toy store?"

"Not really," answered Stripes.

"Nope," Poo-Poo added.

Mutt just shrugged and plopped down onto the ground. His thick, shaggy fur twisted and flopped and shook about before settling.

Stick Dog noticed this.

And Stick Dog had an idea.

"I feel much more positive," he said to Karen. He stretched up a bit and raised his stature. "Thank you for helping me feel better. I feel much less like a, umm, Debbie Downer now. Thank you."

"You're welcome," Karen said proudly.

Stick Dog then turned to Mutt.

"Mutt," he said. "Would you do me a favor?"

"Of course, Stick Dog," Mutt answered. "Anything at all. What can I do for you?"

"Could you give yourself a really good shake?" Stick Dog asked. "Maybe you have something stored in your fur that this little human might enjoy. Something that might make her feel better."

Now, you probably know about Mutt. You probably know that he keeps many, many things in his shaggy fur. Often, some of that stuff has helped the dogs snatch food from humans.

Mutt pushed himself up to standing. He spread his legs a little wider than normal.

Then he shook.

It was a great and vigorous shake.

Several things shot, dropped, and flew from his fur. They included an old sock, a silver bottle cap, one blue mitten with a

chewed-off thumb, a pink eraser, a yellow
pencil stub, an orange straw, and one green
glove with three fingers chewed off.

"Can you believe all that stuff?" Edith said
to Stick Cat. "That dog has awesome fur!
It's not shiny, pristine, and smooth like
mine, mind you. But its stowing capabilities
are spectacular!"

"It's amazing, all right," Stick Cat concurred.
"I just don't know what he's doing. I mean,
what are they going to do with all that
stuff?"

"Beats me," said Edith.

"And how are we going to get Millie home? We still haven't figured that out yet."

"Who knows?" Edith said. "We'll think of something. I'm sure I will anyway. I always have good ideas. We'll just ride it out until we—probably me—come up with something, I guess."

"I hope so."

Just then the dogs answered Stick Cat's earlier question.

Stick Dog picked up the old sock with his mouth and walked slowly toward Millie. He stopped and dropped the sock in front of her.

Karen brought her the silver bottle cap.

Stripes brought the blue mitten.

Poo-Poo brought the pink eraser.

Mutt brought the yellow pencil stub.

"They're bringing her things," Stick Cat said in understanding. "They're giving her stuff to distract her or to play with. They want to make her feel better too. Let's help!"

Stick Cat brought the orange straw to Millie.

Edith brought
the green glove.
It was the last thing.

All of that stuff was scattered about right in front of Millie.

Millie didn't want any of it.

Her eyes welled up more.

Her whimpering got louder. Both cats and all five dogs were disappointed.

Mutt shook a crushed plastic water bottle from his fur and started to chew on it. Chewing on things always made him feel better. When he shook out that water bottle something else fell quietly from his shaggy fur.

Nobody saw it.

Except for Stick Cat.

It was small. One part was hard plastic. The other part was soft rubber. It had a handle.

Stick Cat had seen one just like it every night at bedtime.

In Millie's mouth.

It was the third word she knew.

It was a binkie.

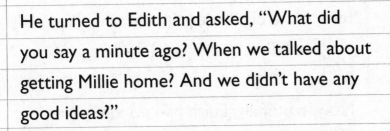

And Stick Cat had an idea.

He turned to Edith and asked, "What did you say a minute ago? When we talked about getting Millie home? And we didn't have any good ideas?"

"I said we'd have to wait until we think of a good idea," answered Edith. "It will likely be me who thinks of it. I have tons of good ideas."

"Yes, I remember," Stick Cat replied, and allowed a slight smile to creep onto his face. His plan had firmed up in his mind. He thought it might—it maybe just might— work. "But it was the *way* you said it. The words you used."

"I said we'd just have to ride it out," remembered Edith. "So what?"

Stick Cat then allowed that slight smile to turn into a big, wide grin. He said, "You did it again, Edith! You figured it out again!"

Now, truthfully, Edith had no idea what Stick Cat was talking about. But that didn't matter. This had happened before. She was

all too happy to take credit for the idea—
whatever it was.

"Well, of course I did, Stick Cat," she said
proudly. "Don't I always?"

"Yes, you do, Edith," Stick Cat said as he
walked toward Mutt. "Yes, you do."

 Stick Cat picked up the
binkie by the handle with
his mouth. He walked past
Millie with it.

He didn't give it to her. But he made sure
she saw it.

Millie stopped whimpering. She exclaimed,
"Binkie!"

She followed Stick Cat immediately.

For his plan to work, Stick Cat needed
one thing to happen. But he had no idea
if it actually *would* happen. He needed the
dogs' leader—the really smart one—to
understand what he was doing.

"Hey, Stick Dog," Poo-Poo called. "That
male cat is coming toward you. He's got
some weird plastic thing in his mouth."

Stick Dog tilted his head a bit.
He observed the cat getting
closer. He saw the little human
following the cat. She had
stopped making that sad sound.

"Please understand," Stick Cat, with the
binkie in his mouth, mumble-whispered to
the dog. "Please understand."

Stick Dog watched as the cat walked
around to his left side. He heard him meow
a couple of times—but he, of course, didn't
understand cat language.

Stick Dog watched the little human
approach him from the other side.

He saw the cat hold up that plastic object.

He saw the little human's eyes open wide.
He saw her smile and reach out.

Stick Dog dropped down to his belly.

Stick Dog understood.

Chapter 25

SLEEPY TIME

Stick Cat stood up on his hind legs, leaning gently against the left side of the dog's body. The dog didn't mind at all.

Stick Cat held the binkie up in the air above the dog's back.

Millie reached for the binkie, leaning gently against the dog's right side.

Stick Dog didn't mind at all.

Stick Cat pulled the binkie back a bit—out of Millie's reach.

Millie climbed up onto the dog's back.

Stick Dog didn't mind at all.

Stick Cat allowed Millie to reach the binkie.

"Binkie!"

Millie put it in her mouth and lay down on Stick Dog's back.

She closed her eyes.

She went to sleep.

And Stick Dog didn't mind at all.

Chapter 26

STICK DOG UNDERSTANDS

"She's asleep!" Edith said happily. "That's a good thing. That part of my plan obviously worked. But how do we get her home? How does that part of my plan work?"

"She's going to ride out, just like you suggested," Stick Cat said.

"Jeez, I sure do come up with good plans, don't I?" Edith asked. "I'm quite the genius."

"You certainly are," agreed Stick Cat. "Now we just need that smart dog to follow us back home."

Stick Cat walked to the edge of the clearing.
He could see their house. It wasn't far away.
He looked over his shoulder back at the dog
and meowed.

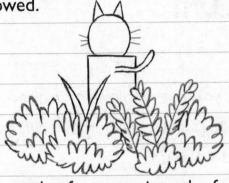

Stick Cat took a few steps into the forest—
the first few steps home.

He stopped and looked over
his shoulder again.

Stick Dog—and Millie—were
right behind him.

Stick Dog understood.

Chapter 27

BACON!

Now, you might think a two-year-old sleeping on a dog's back walking through the forest would wake up.

But you're forgetting how you slept when you were two years old. Of course you don't remember. Nobody remembers anything from when they were two years old.

And who would want to anyway?

I mean, mushy baby food? Falling down all the time? Diapers?

Who wants to remember that stuff?

But if you could remember, you would know
that two-year-olds sleep really deeply. They
are O-U-T, out. Like unconscious. A two-
year-old can sleep through a thunderstorm.
Or a jumbo jet landing on the driveway.
Heck, I bet if you dribbled a sleeping
two-year-old like a basketball, she wouldn't
wake up.

Don't do that!

Don't dribble a
sleeping two-year-old.

BAD
IDEA

That would be bad.

I'm just saying two-year-olds never wake up
until they are ready to wake up.

Millie slept the whole way through the forest on Stick Dog's back. She slept all the way across the backyard. She slept as they all squeezed between the slats of the backyard fence. She slept when Stick Dog lay down next to the Door of Freedom.

She slept as Stick Cat slid her off Stick Dog's back. She slept as Stick Cat pulled and Edith pushed her through that door. She slept as they dragged and shoved her under the kitchen table. She actually slid quite easily on the smooth kitchen floor.

She slept when Edith curled up beside her and went instantly—and deeply—asleep too.

She even slept when Stick Cat reached that plate piled high with bacon off the kitchen counter. It banged a little bit when he pushed it outside to give to those five friendly, hungry dogs.

Those dogs LOVED that bacon.

And Stick Cat loved sharing it with them.

Chapter 28

HOME

The dogs had just left the backyard when Tiffany pulled her car into the driveway.

Stick Cat watched as she came through the door with a bag of groceries.

"Goose!" she called. "Can you help me with the bags?"

"On my way," Goose called back.

Stick Cat watched as they spent a few minutes bringing more bags in. He watched as they discovered Millie and Edith sleeping under the table.

Tiffany thought Goose had put Millie there
for a nap while she was at the store. And
Goose thought Tiffany had put her there
when she got back from the store.

But Stick Cat knew better.

Stick Cat always knew better.

THE END

Tom Watson is the author of the Stick Dog series.
There are currently nine books in that series—and
more to come.

He lives in Chicago with his wife, daughter, and son.
He also has a dog, as you could probably guess. The dog
is a Labrador-Newfoundland mix. Tom says he looks like
a Labrador with a bad perm. He wanted to name the
dog "Put Your Shirt On" (please don't ask why), but he
was outvoted by his family. The dog's name is Shadow.
Shadow gives Tom lots of ideas for the Stick Dog series.

Tom Watson is also the author of the Stick Cat series.

Tom does not have a cat. So his ideas for the Stick Cat
series come from a whole different place. He's not sure
where that place is exactly, but he knows it's kind of
strange there.

Visit him online at stickdogbooks.com!

Also available as an ebook.

STICK WITH READING!

Pick up these animal adventures by Tom Watson today!

Visit www.stickdogbooks.com for
teaching guides, videos, activities, and more!

HARPER

An Imprint of HarperCollinsPublishers

www.harpercollinschildrens.